# TONI MOUNT

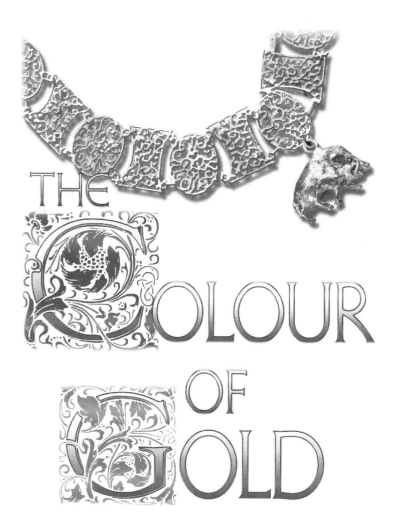

# THE COLOUR OF GOLD

# The Colour of Gold

A Sebastian Foxley Medieval Mystery
Book 2

Copyright © 2017 Toni Mount
ISBN-13: 978-84-946498-0-6

## M
MadeGlobal Publishing

For more information on
MadeGlobal Publishing, visit
our website
www.madeglobal.com

# Dedication

For Bethan, Owen and Isaac

# *PROLOGUE*

THE CHAPEL lay silent in the night, like one who slumbered in the light of a few torches. The scent of incense and old parchment was its coverlet, the alabaster images of saints its bed-mates. Footsteps, more quiet than a cat upon velvet paws, crossed the tiles to a saint's niche. Secreted behind a curtain, St Peter stood enrobed in darkness, but such nimble hands had no need of light to find what they sought. A weighty chain hung about the saint's shoulders and, heavy though it was, it proved the task of a moment to lift it off. Then the footsteps retreated into the night, leaving St Peter naked of his fine collar of goldsmith's work.

# A Short Story of
## Fifteenth-Century London Folk

**B**OTH SEBASTIAN Foxley and his brother, Jude, were but recently made Freemen of the Stationers' Company in London and set-up in business in Paternoster Row, in the same premises as they had lately been journeymen. It was a tradition among the stationers that a freeman of the guild, upon his wedding day, should wear the gold livery chain, bequeathed a decade since in the will of Sir Ralph Fabyan, a former Warden of the Company. The chain was kept in St Faith's Chapel, hung about the neck of the stationers' patron saint, St Peter, within his curtained niche. After the generous legacy had been made known, the right to possess the heavy gold collar, with the enamelled company arms pendant, had been briefly contested by Sir Ralph's son, Henry, in the Court of Hustings which dealt with such matters in the city. But the stationers had been adjudged the rightful recipients and there was an end to it.

'It's a fine piece, little brother,' Jude had said on Sunday morn, after High Mass, as they stood in the chapel, inspecting St Peter's adornment. Jude tested its weight in his hand. 'It'll look well around your skinny neck, though I dare say it'll be too bloody heavy for you to wear for long. After all, you'll need to keep all your strength up for the nuptial bedding ceremony after, won't you?' he laughed, clapping Seb on the back harder than necessary.

Seb gave him a rueful smile that set Jude laughing anew.

'You're not looking forward to that part of the day, are you? Why? Afeared you might disappoint your bride, are you? A fine specimen of manhood such as you. Unless you would have me take your place in the darkness? Or do you fear I'll loosen the ropes on the bridal bed and have you fall through?'

'Don't jest about it, please.'

Seb knew only too well that his gangly frame and uneven gait hardly made him a prize worthy of the most beguiling lass in the city, but that was women for you – forever beyond the comprehension of mere men. Emily Appleyard had agreed to marry him. Not the handsome, lusty Jude, but meek and mild Sebastian Foxley. A mystery indeed. He liked to think she valued his talents as an artist and illuminator of manuscripts. The fact that the Duke of Gloucester was his patron probably added to his meagre attractions, not forgetting that he had rescued Emily from a fate worse than death at the hands of Lord Lovell not so long ago. Did those things pass for love in a woman's mind, he wondered.

'I've failed you, little brother, I realise that now,' Jude was saying. 'I should have found a comely whore or two to educate you. But it's not too late. There's always tonight.'

'No. Certainly not. I'll not go to my bride's bed stinking of a brothel with another woman's sweat upon my skin.'

'Yer can always keep yer shirt on, master,' Jack suggested, 'Wiv the 'ore, I mean, so yer don't get her stink on yer.'

'What would you know of such matters, young Jack?' Seb asked their scruffy, one-time street urchin turned apprentice – of sorts – of indeterminate age.

'I knowed lots of 'ores, didn't I? They used to share stuff wot I stoled, pies an' fruit an' fings an' in return, some of 'em would lend us a blanket at night when it wos cold. An' lots of 'em didn't stink at all. They wos kind t' me, wosn't they?'

Jack reached out with sticky fingers to touch the chain.

'Leave it,' Jude said. 'Remember, I know your old ways well enough. Don't you dare touch it.'

'I wos on'y gonna...

'Aye. You were only going to dust off the bloody cobwebs.'

'Well, it is filfy, ent it?'

'We can dust it on the morrow, afore I wear it,' Seb said. 'Now, come. There is much else still to be done, not least I must collect the ring from the goldsmith.'

Jude closed the curtain, returning St Peter to his secluded gloom.

• •

It was a good day for a wedding: Monday, the second day of October in the year of Our Lord 1475. Seb and his bride-to-be had chosen the date in honour of their very special guest, Richard, Duke of Gloucester, whose birthday it was. To wed upon a Monday was also supposed to guarantee wealth for the happy couple.

The marriage notice had been pinned up, as the law required, in the church porch of St Michael le Querne in Cheapside, their parish for most of their lives, and also in the Chapel of Saint Faith under St Paul's Cathedral, it being the parish church of the Worshipful Company of Stationers. No one had come forth to proclaim any objection to their union, so the great day was eagerly anticipated by all. The duke, being conveniently in London upon some private business matter, had accepted the invitation, much to everyone's surprise, and now the folk of two parishes were in a turmoil of feverish preparations, to ensure that the ceremony at St Paul's and the subsequent feasting and celebration were worthy of so illustrious a royal guest.

Before dawn upon that Monday, up in the chamber they shared above the workshop in Paternoster Row, Seb and Jude had both washed thoroughly, from head to toe, having carted two buckets of hot water, the latter scented with rosewater, from the kitchen and up the outside wooden stairs. This was the last time Seb would sleep here. Tonight he would be in the bridal bed, in the chamber across the yard.

Seb's dark hair was still dripping as Jude lit an extra taper before setting about shaving his brother's chin with a fine honed blade.

'Are you nervous?' Jude asked.

'A little.'

'Don't move your mouth when I'm shaving your chin, you fool.'

'You did ask.'

'Now, look. I near cut your lip.' He wiped his brother's face with a wash cloth to remove what he had shaven off. 'There. I made a good job of that, Seb. Now you can return the favour. And don't nick my chin, whatever you do. I don't want blood spots on my new doublet... it cost me a damn fortune. And all in your honour, too.'

'Aye, 'tis very fine, Jude. You will outshine me, as always. That crimson hue suits you very well, indeed.' Seb stroked the blade down his elder brother's cheek with utmost care. 'And I envy you that feathered cap, too.'

'Mm, I believe I made a most excellent choice in that. The black plume is from an osteridge bird, or some such. Did you know that?'

'No, I never heard of the creature. Where do they dwell?'

'Paradise, so the tailor told me.'

'Little wonder that it cost so much, then. You can move now. I've finished shaving you.'

Jude ran his hands over his cheeks.

'You missed a bristle here.'

'No, I didn't. 'Tis a mole you have always had.'

'Oh. It doesn't mar my looks, does it?'

'Fear not, you are still the best-looking fellow in London, Jude. Now, where is Jack?' Seb went to the door. 'Jack! These water buckets can be emptied now, if you will?' Then he began searching around the chamber, a frantic look upon his face. The beds and coffers were strewn with items of clothing – mostly Jude's. He was an untidy room-mate.

'What have you lost, little brother?'

'The ring. I cannot recall where...'

'You gave it to me, remember?' Jude held out a small leather pouch. 'Do you think I would lose the most expensive thing you've ever bought? I just hope she's worth it.'

'Of course Emily is worth it. She's the most precious thing to me and deserves the best I can afford.'

Jude opened the pouch, took out the ring and held it to the candlelight. The sapphire stone, a symbol of faithfulness, glinted darkly.

'Well crafted, I grant you,' he said, squinting at the goldsmith's workmanship. 'You're sure 'tis true gold?' He was about to test it with his teeth.

'Don't spoil it, I beg you. Most certainly it is gold. Master Edmund be of good repute.'

'Aye, but it's just as well to be sure.' Jude returned the ring to its bag and tucked it into his purse for safe-keeping. 'And what shall you be wearing, Seb? Your usual old tunic and jerkin, no doubt?'

Jude went to the linen press to take out their freshly laundered shirts, but caught his foot against one of the water buckets, slopping water over his naked feet. 'Where's bloody Jack got to? Why hasn't he removed these? And it wouldn't hurt if he washed himself in them first.'

'He won't do that unless we force him. You know his fear of bathing.'

'Aye, but the dirty little bugger could make the effort, just this once. We can see to it that he's clean. Dunk him in the bucket.' Jude opened the chamber door. 'Jack!' he bellowed, 'Get your idle backside in here, damn it.'

Tom Bowen, their official apprentice, appeared instead, coming down from the attic he and Jack shared.

'Sorry, masters,' he said, yawning and running his fingers through his sleep-tousled hair. 'Jack was up and out hours since. I fear I went back to sleep.'

'Well, get decent and empty these bloody buckets.'

Tom sighed. An apprentice, registered and indentured as he was to Master Seb, wasn't supposed to be required to do such menial tasks but he knew better than to argue with Master Jude. He didn't want to attend the wedding with a throbbing ear, all red and swollen.

Having assisted his brother in tying the points that fastened his close-fitting black hose to his pourpoint of fine Holland linen, Seb stepped back to admire Jude. The black hose were the latest fashion from Burgundy.

'Now the doublet,' he said. As intended by the wearer, the dark hose showed off to perfection Jude's doublet of crimson wool. Finished off with his red boots and the black velvet hat with its beautiful plume set upon his golden hair, Jude cut quite a dash. 'You look splendid, indeed,' Seb said, sighing, knowing he could never be other than his brother's pale shadow.

'Good. And I'm only the groom's man. What about you, little brother? Let's get you dressed.'

Seb opened his clothes coffer – compared to Jude's, it was nigh empty – and took out his best hose.

'Lord's sake, Seb, you can't wear those. You'll bloody embarrass me.' Jude held aloft the grey hose to show the repairs made to them at one time or another.'

'The darning is neatly done. Em did them for me.'

'I don't care if the Virgin Mary darned them for you, my brother is not going to his own wedding wearing mended hose. So 'tis as well that I bought a second pair of black ones, isn't it?'

'Oh, no, Jude. I cannot wear any so tightly shaped and black. Everyone will notice my legs, the way I walk. No, the grey will do me well enough.'

'They will not and don't argue.'

'Please, Jude.'

Jude took out the little knife he used to shape his quills and stabbed the blade into one leg of the hose before ripping it in twain.

'Jude! My hose. My best hose.'

'Now you have no choice. Wear the black or go bare-arsed before the duke.'

'Jude, that is not fair.'

But Jude shrugged, holding out the fine new ones.

Knowing there was no help for it, Seb pulled on the hose. The cloth felt silky smooth against his skin. There was no denying Jude understood the selection and buying of cloth better than most, but Seb so hated to be noticed, wearing such garments went against his nature. At least his shirt was of good stuff. Jude could not complain about that, but his old faded green doublet was another case entirely. Jude was going to disapprove of it, he knew, and would ridicule him for wearing something that had lain in the coffer for years, a cast-off of their father's waiting until one of them should grow into it. Of course, it had never been worn by Jude – too unfashionable and bedevilled by moths for that – but it suited Seb well enough on the rare occasions when a doublet was required.

Seb shook off the dried lavender flowers that kept his clothes sweet-smelling and held up the doublet. A half year since its last wearing had not improved it. In places, the once dark green cloth had faded to near yellow, the moth-holes were more numerous, despite the lavender that was supposed to keep them at bay, and it was frayed at the neck and hem worse than he remembered. Too late now. He turned from the coffer to find Jude standing behind him, grinning like a king's fool, displaying a garment across his arm.

'What do you think, little brother?' he asked, holding out a fine doublet. 'Nigh fit for a duke, is it not?'

Seb looked at the sad, once-green doublet that he held and then at Jude.

'Aye, but 'tis too good for a humble man.'

'It's yours Seb. I had it made, knowing otherwise you'd go to your nuptials looking worse than a bloody beggar. See? 'Tis fine tabby-weave wool, dyed with the best blue dye and trimmed with marten fur. The latest style with slashed sleeves to show the lining of scarlet. You will be dressed as a man of account for this day at least, come what may, if I have to dose you with a sleeping potion in order to get you into it. Now put it on, or do I have to make dire threats against your person? Besides, you can't wear the stationers' gold livery chain over some tattered rags, now can you? It would insult the company. Speaking of which...'

• •

Tom went straight to the dean's vestry in St Paul's, chinking the purse Master Seb had given him. Twelve pence: a whole shilling. It seemed a large sum to pay for the wearing of a chain for a few hours, even a gold one. But who was he to question it? Apparently, the coins went to pay a priest to say masses for the departed soul of the man who had bequeathed the chain for any freeman of the company to wear for his bridal day. One day, Tom thought, mayhap he would get to wear it. He knocked upon the oak door. After a time of waiting, he knocked again.

'What?' The plump cleric, obviously not the dean, who opened the door at last was less than courteous, seeing a lad, however respectably attired, come to disturb his breakfast. 'What is it you want?' he said, dabbing at his mouth with the table napkin he still held.

'Master Sebastian Foxley has sent me. Today being his marrying day, he is permitted to wear the Stationers' Company livery chain. The Warden of the Company, Master Richard Collop, awaits us in St Faith's Chapel with my master.'

'Go, tell your master to come himself, *after* I have finished my breakfast.'

'I have the money,' Tom said, rattling the purse.

'Why didn't you say before, instead of wasting my precious time?' The cleric dropped his napkin on the floor and kicked it aside before snatching the purse, which promptly disappeared within the folds of his cassock. 'You think I have nought better to do than run around, fetching and carrying for some wretched guild with its ridiculous traditions? Well, come along, hasten then.'

The cleric strode off at quite a pace, muttering under his breath, his sandals slapping on the black and white tiles. Tom hurried after him, towards the ancient stone steps that led down to the crypt of the great cathedral. The steps were so worn with age, each had been scooped out in a half-moon shape by the passage of nigh a thousand years' worth of pilgrims' feet, come to seek blessing.

The crypt was lit by torches in cressets, such that anyone wishing to pray in St Faith's vaulted chapel – or in the case of many local stationers, come to collect from their stores of paper, kept there under the guardianship of their especial saint – might see their way. St Peter gazed solemnly upon those of the trade who would offer him their prayers or beg his intercession with the Almighty. Tom always thought the saint didn't look to be of a humour to aid anyone, so stern was his expression. The Keeper of the Keys of Heaven made him feel guilty of some transgression, even if he wasn't.

Masters Seb and Jude waited before the niche with old Richard Collop, the stationer with whom Master Seb had served his apprenticeship. Now he was Warden of the Company and here in that capacity to place the gold livery chain about the bridegroom's neck.

The plump cleric, sighing audibly, withdrew the velvet curtain and Master Jude held close a candle to set before the grumpy looking saint. And this day St Peter appeared more sour and affronted than usual, as well he might.

The handsome golden livery chain that should have encompassed his neck was gone.

'You have removed it already,' the cleric said, scowling. 'I've been dragged down here for no good reason.'

The three stationers and the apprentice stood in silence, staring at the statue.

'No, sir,' Warden Collop said at last, 'I swear to you, no one has touched it as yet, certainly not with the company's permission. I fear it has been stolen.' The old man turned to his one-time apprentice. 'I am so sorry, Sebastian. Of course, I will order the theft be looked into but, in the meantime, sadly, it seems you must wed without the distinction of wearing Sir Ralph's chain. I am sorry,' he repeated, touching Seb's arm in a gesture of consolation.

Seb nodded.

'Aye. But the marriage will still have the guild's blessing?'

'Of course. No doubt about that, Sebastian,' said Warden Collop.

'Then all is not lost. Besides, the ceremony is not to begin until eleven of the clock so we have above two hours to find the chain. Come Jude, Tom, we have a thief to uncover.'

• •

'I shouldn't be searching in such dirty places in my new doublet,' Jude complained as he sorted through a pile of parchment rolls that had lain unused for years in a corner of the vaulted chapel. 'I swear these haven't been looked at since King John sealed the Magna Carta. Look at how the dust shows on my black hose! They're bloody ruined now. And what makes you think this damned chain is here, anyway?'

'Nought but the fact we must begin somewhere. You said yourself, yesterday, how heavy it was, so mayhap it hasn't been carried too far.' Seb wiped away a cobweb that had dragged across his face.

'But why remove it only to leave it behind? I tell you, Seb, we won't find the chain here.'

'Then where? If you have some better idea where we might search, then say.'

Tom gave a hefty sneeze as he disturbed a cloud of dust from a stack of paper.

'I reckon the thief would sell it, master,' he said, sniffing and sneezing again. 'Sorry. I forgot my kerchief, master. Do you have one I could use?'

Seb handed him a square of linen.

'Young Jack would no doubt have some knowledge on such matters. Where is he? I haven't seen him all morn.'

'Nor I,' said Tom. 'Oh, no, I've rent my hose...'

'I'm grateful for Jack's absence,' said Jude, ignoring Seb and Tom's bewailing of the ruination of the lad's attire. 'How peaceful it is without him whining and whingeing and getting into scrapes. And we will be better served at the wedding breakfast without that flea-bitten mongrel of his shitting everywhere.'

'You don't think we have cause to worry about Jack, then?'

'No, little brother. Let's concern ourselves with finding this bloody chain. Jack can take care of himself, as he always did afore I was fool enough to take him in, off the streets. *Mea culpa*, I know. We could always put the little bugger back where he came from.' Jude climbed down from a ladder propped against a teetering pile of oak book boards and dusted off his doublet with hands so dirty they made things worse. 'Damn it, Seb. If the chain is here, it can bloody stay where it lies. I'm done getting filthy in my best clothes and there's an end to it. Let's go home. I'm in need of some ale to wash this dust from my mouth.'

• •

Back home, in the kitchen, Seb, Jude and young Tom sat over their cups of ale.

'We cannot afford to waste time in this manner,' Seb said, draining his ale in a few mouthfuls, 'Come, we must keep looking.'

'Aye, so you insist but where would you have us look, eh? Would you have us search the entire cathedral when the bloody chain could be anywhere in the city... or even beyond? And look at the state of us. We're hardly fit company for the duke any longer.'

''Tis but dust, Jude. It will brush off.'

'Speak for yourself. I have cobwebs in my hair, pigeon shit on my boots and candle grease on my new doublet and as for Tom... just look at his hose: they're ripped into holes.' Jude emptied his cup and refilled it from the jug. 'Go change your hose, lad. Duke Richard can't see your bloody knees poking through like that.'

'But I only have my workaday hose apart from these. These are my Sunday best.'

'*Were* your Sunday best, I fear. You'll have to wear the others.'

Tom stumped out of the kitchen and across the yard, his mood evident in the heaviness of his tread up the wooden steps to the attic room, which could be heard in the kitchen.

'Seb, this damned chain is more trouble than it's worth. You'll just have to get wed without the bloody thing. No one will notice anyway, once the drink starts flowing. No one will care so long as the food is plentiful.'

'Aye. You be right, Jude. Who needs a gold livery collar to make the day special? Everyone will be too entranced by the bride's beauty – and your dazzling attire, of course – to even notice me.'

'My dazzling attire, indeed! Fetch me some clean water and a sponge, will you? I must try to do what I can with this doublet. How does a house of God get to be so filthy? Do they never clean it?'

'I be so sorry for this, Jude. I never meant for so much trouble to...'

'Sorry isn't going to help now, is it? Get me the white vinegar, see if that'll work.'

• •

'Master Seb! Master Jude!' Tom came rushing into the kitchen, wearing but a single holey stocking.

'I told you to change,' Jude said.

'But look! I found it. I found the chain, masters, except that...' Tom held out the livery collar.

'Where was it? Where did you find it?' Seb asked, all eager now, a bright smile upon his lips. He was nigh dancing a joyous jig about the kitchen, holding high his prize.

'It was in our clothes coffer; me and Jack's, though most of the stuff is mine. It was buried right at the bottom where I kept my old hose but I know not how it got there. You must believe me, masters.'

'How it got there, matters not. At least I can wear it now.'

'I'm not so sure, Seb,' Jude said, frowning at the chain. He took it from his brother and went to the door, to examine it in a better light. 'This isn't it. It isn't even gold. Look at it!'

'But it's the company's livery collar,' Seb said. 'Of course it's gold. It must be.'

'Well, if it is the company's collar, they've been deceived all these years. 'Tis but gilded lead – a tawdry thing. A bloody fake.'

'No. It cannot be.'

'See for yourself, little brother.' Jude gave him the chain. 'Scrape your nail upon the gold and it comes off. 'Tis shoddy workmanship. You can make out where some of the links have been scoured and the thin veneer of gold is worn away, to show the grey metal beneath. It is a fake and not a very good one at that.'

Seb threw the chain on the board and sat down heavily upon a stool, his shoulders slumped.

'What am I going to tell Warden Collop and the company? How do I explain that a fake version of their gold collar is found in our house? They will conclude that one of us stole the genuine one and we have tried to replace it with a cheap substitute. Oh, Jude, what am I going to do? They will denounce us for certain.'

'Wot's de-nunce mean, master?' asked a small voice from the doorstep.

'Jack! Where have you been, lad? We were concerned for you,' Seb said. 'You have little time to wash and put on those clothes that Dame Ellen sent for you to wear at the wedding. Make haste, now.'

But Jack was not listening. He stared at the table board and what lay there, discarded. With a long, shuddering breath, the lad turned and fled out into yard, tears coursing down his grubby face.

'Well,' said Jude, 'I think we have just found our thief, betrayed by his own tears, the little bugger. I've always known he would bring us nought but trouble.'

'This makes no sense, Jude. Of what use is the chain to Jack?'

'He could sell it, same as any other thing he ever stole.'

'Yet he promised me: no more thievery.'

'And more fool you for believing his promise. He was born a thief and a liar. What else can be expected of his kind? They know no better. An empty promise made to be broken; a string of meaningless words is all it is to him. Forget him, Seb. He isn't worth the bloody effort.'

'I would know why, Jude,' Seb said, following Jack. 'Help me catch him, Tom, you can run faster.'

'Sorry, Master Seb, I am but half dressed,' Tom reminded him, showing one naked leg.

'No one is going to waste their time chasing an unholy urchin but you, Seb,' Jude said. 'Forget him. We have a wedding to go to, remember, if my doublet dries out in time. Tom, put some bloody hose on. My eyes are sore, being nigh blinded by that lily-white arse of yours.'

• •

The weather was fine. The morning mist had lifted and St Paul's Yard was lapped in autumnal sunshine, turning the cathedral stone to palest gold. As a freeman of the city, it was Seb's privilege to be wed at Paul's door. He had decided to wear the fake collar, realising that not to do so would cause the greater controversy.

When he arrived with Jude at the porch, many of their friends and neighbours were already there, including the Duke of Gloucester and Sir Robert Percy. The brothers went straight to greet their most important guests, bending the knee before Lord Richard.

'Up, up, Masters Foxley. Do not spoil such fine hose in the dirt. Of Burgundian cut, are they not?' the duke said, putting them at their ease. 'And good weather for the occasion, too.' He eyed the cloudless sky appreciatively.

'Forgive us for not being here upon your arrival, your grace, but there was some delay over this livery collar,' Seb explained. His hands, of their own accord, went to cover the pendant, lying dull upon his chest.

'Indeed. It had come to my ears that the bridegroom, by tradition, wears a fine gold chain. Did I mishear?' The duke bent to see the chain more closely.

'No, my lord, you heard aright but, sadly, the chain in question has proved to be rather less than its reputation claimed.'

Sir Robert also peered at the offending collar.

'If I may make so bold a suggestion, master,' he said, 'And I understand if you refuse my offer as breaking with tradition, but would my Yorkist livery chain not look better? Begging my lord's permission, of course.'

Seb smiled broadly, feeling his heart lift. He was not happy to have the nasty fake about his person yet felt he had to wear something.

'That would be a great honour, sir, and such a kindness, if my lord allows?'

'Nay. I would not have it so,' said the duke, sounding stern. Then he grinned. 'Sir Robert's chain is of silver gilt and, I believe, the tradition says it should be of gold? In which case, I think it more appropriate that the groom, since I am his patron, should wear my livery chain of gold.' With that, Lord Richard removed his own Yorkist collar and put it about Seb's neck, replacing the fake. 'There. Much better.'

'M-my lord, I-I don't know... I hardly...' Seb tried to object but seeing a glint of steel in the duke's eye, thought better of protesting. 'I am greatly honoured, my lord, and humbly give you my thanks.'

• •

Seb felt the October sun warm upon his back as he stood outside the porch, waiting. And the wait seemed long indeed. Nervous humours were threatening to get the better of him. Would she come? Or would he have to explain to the Duke of Gloucester and all these guests that Emily Appleyard had regained her sense of reason and come to realise her mistake. That there was to be no wedding this day after all. He fidgeted with his new doublet, retying the lacings, pulling it straight, adjusting the slashed sleeves and fiddling with the boar pendant on the duke's livery collar.

'For pity's sake, Seb, let it be, can't you?' Jude said, pulling his brother's twitching fingers from the pendant. 'Your doublet looks perfect. Don't ruin it.'

'She's isn't going to come, is she? I know it.'

'Of course she'll bloody come, little brother, if only so as not to miss her chance to see the duke. Fear not, she'll be here. Christ knows, she barely has to walk a few dozen steps from her father's house to get here. The bride is supposed to be late. Now cease fretting. And leave those damned lacings alone.'

'Have you got the ring safe?'

'Aye. I've got it. You think I might have mislaid it since you last asked me a few moments ago? Stop fidgeting, can't you? You're making me anxious.'

'Supposing she has had second thoughts. What then?'

'Supposing you stop chewing your nails afore you make them bleed? I've never known you in such a dither before.'

'Well, I never got married before, did I? I wish we could just go home. I wish we'd never invited all these folk. I wish...'

'Seb. You're annoying me. Now be quiet and wait patiently. She'll be here, I promise you.'

'But what if...'

Then a cheer was raised, fit to rattle the stained-glass windows, as the bridal party appeared in solemn procession around the western end of the great cathedral.

Seb was so relieved, his sigh audible to those beside him.

Jude squeezed his shoulder in a gesture that said 'I told you so'.

Young Nessie, never renowned for her nimbleness, had yet insisted she could walk backwards all the way before the bride, strewing dried lavender and clean-scented marigold petals in her path. It was as well that, with forethought, Jude had paid some local lads a penny each to clear the streets along the route and Paul's Yard of their usual foul litter of rubbish and dung.

Beneath the embroidered bridal canopy, sewn by her own hand, Emily walked beside her father, Stephen Appleyard, wearing his official city livery as Warden Archer. Her younger brother John, Churchwarden Marlowe and two neighbours each carried a pole, supporting the canopy. Following behind was Father Thomas from St Michael's with Dame Ellen Langton, who was taking the part of the bride's mother – even down to the copious tears – and a gaggle of women as supporters of the bride. All were decked in their finery, reds and greens, yellows and blues, even fur and jewels, enough to tempt the sheriff into fining them for exceeding their status, according to the sumptuary laws. But today, no one cared a jot for such foolish rulings.

Seb stood proudly beside Jude. He hardly dared look at Emily, unsure whether he could govern his feelings if he did. He wanted to shout for joy and burst into tears of relief that she was here, yet feared he might just laugh out loud if she smiled back at him. From the corner of his eye he caught glimpses of her fair, braided hair covered in a fine mesh of gold thread, her gown of a hue that matched his doublet. Was that a coincidence or no? He remembered to stand tall and upright. Only a few months ago, his misshapen shoulder and hip would never have permitted this stance. Now, much recovered from his afflictions, one leg still felt a little awkward, forcing him to adopt a slightly lop-sided position he hoped others wouldn't notice, but certain his new hose must exaggerate his somewhat wasted calf muscle.

Between them, Father Thomas stood ready to conduct the sacrament of holy wedlock, wearing his new-fangled spectacles to help him read the text from the well-thumbed book. After a few opening words in Latin that only the duke, Sir Robert and most of the stationers could comprehend, the priest began the important part of the ceremony, in English. Else few would know what was said as the young couple made their vows, least of all the bride.

Seb felt a shiver of anticipation run through him at the moment when Stephen Appleyard placed his daughter's hand in his, symbolising the passing of a father's responsibility to the husband. Emily's life was now his. Was he sufficient to the task? He held her left hand gently in his right, their fingers intertwined, a delicate gesture of a future life together.

Jude placed the ring – in no way mislaid – upon the priest's open book. Father Thomas blessed it and held out the book for Seb to take the ring. Knowing his hand was shaking, he feared he might drop it and see it roll away, but he braced himself and accomplished the placing of the sapphire on Emily's finger without mishap.

The priest now wound his stole about their linked hands and announced to the crowd, that all might know: 'Those whom the Lord God hath bound together in the bond of holy matrimony let no man upon earth dare to put asunder.' Then he turned to Seb, an expectant look upon his face. 'Well, go on, my son, you may now kiss the bride.'

Seb was seized by a momentary panic but Emily took his face in both her hands and kissed him hard and long upon the lips, encouraged by the friendly ribaldry of the crowd. Cheers resounded from the walls enclosing St Paul's Yard and the deed was done. For better or for worse, Seb Foxley and Emily Appleyard were married.

Then there was an unseemly rush as every man, bar the duke, old or young, single, wedded or celibate, came to demand his bridal kiss.

Dame Ellen went among the guests, offering a tray of biscuits freshly baked in Pudding Lane, and the colourful crowd started to make their way to the celebration breakfast in St Michael's.

• •

The trestles and boards for the nuptial breakfast had been set up in the nave of St Michael le Querne's church. The upper board was laid before the Rood Screen and the rest of the tables ran down the two sides of the nave between the wooden pillars that supported the roof. Golden wheat ears and ruby red rose hips, entwined among long lengths of ivy and coloured ribbons to decorate the little church. The boards were clothed in snowy linen cloths but, in truth, the linen was barely seen beneath the platters, dishes and bowls, all piled high with food. A succulent roasted boar's head – the duke's gift – steamed upon a silver charger, given a small table all of its own, awaiting the attentions of his lordship's personal carver for the occasion and dear friend, Sir Robert. The scent of meat and spices had mouths watering and bellies rumbling in anticipation.

A chair had been placed at the centre of the board – the seat of honour for the duke – with stools for the bridal couple set on either side. But Lord Richard had other ideas. It broke the rules of etiquette, but who would dare gainsay a royal duke, except the king himself? With a wink at Seb and a wide grin, Lord Richard ordered his chair exchanged with the bridegroom's stool.

'Who am I to deny Our Lord God's own ordinance that those whom He hath joined together in holy matrimony, no man may come betwixt?' Lord Richard laughed, seeing Seb's expression of utter surprise. 'But first, I would claim my rightful kiss from the bride – with your permission of course, Master Sebastian.'

Seb nodded, as if there was any possibility of refusing.

Lord Richard made a proper job of it too, taking the bride in his arms and pressing his lips to hers as heartily as any other of the lusty young men present would wish to do, if they dared. Everyone cheered and applauded. Seb looked away, admiring the autumn garlands hung along the nave in celebration of the day. Some of the leaves showed such splendid hues, did they not?

'Come, take your seat, I pray you, Master Sebastian,' the duke said, stepping away from Emily and pulling out the chair for Seb, just as a servant would.

Once seated though, being so honoured caused Seb to wonder now at what courtesy required of him. Should he speak with the duke, whom he could hardly ignore? Yet the new seating arrangement made it the case that he now shared his platter with his bride. He wondered if Emily was disappointed at not having Lord Richard beside her, sharing his meat.

Yet he should have known the duke would make matters simple for him. Lord Richard was soon in conversation with Jude on his right hand with much laughter ensuing, leaving Seb to give his bride his fullest attention.

When Father Thomas completed the saying of grace with a few brief Latin phrases, Sir Rob carved the boar before the top table, piling the juiciest, most tender morsels upon a chased silver dish that he then offered to the duke on bended knee. The duke waved it away with his hand.

'Courtesy, Sir Robert. Where be your manners? Serve those of highest estate first,' he ordered, a twinkle of mischief in his steel-grey eyes.

'Of course, my lord. How remiss of me.' Sir Rob held out the dish to Seb, who took but two small morsels to put upon his platter, offering the choicest to Emily on his knife. Sir Rob leaned close and used his carver's knife to heap more meat on the bridal plate. 'You two will need more than that to see you through the day. Remember how the evening has to be concluded.'

Emily blushed as red as Jude's boots.

'Thank you, sir. I haven't forgotten,' she whispered, fluttering her eyelashes and making him laugh.

'Em, you be as bad as the rest of them,' Seb muttered.

'Lord's sake, Seb, it's our wedding day. Enjoy it, can't you? 'Tis all in jest.'

Seb wasn't so sure. Glancing down the table to his right, Lord Richard and Jude were obviously deep in mirth together. Were they amused at the thought of him making a fool of himself later in the bridal bed? To his left, beyond Emily, her father, Stephen Appleyard, handsome in his official livery as Warden Archer, was likewise enjoying his conversation with Warden Collop and Dame Ellen Langton. All smiles – but with furtive sidelong glances at him. He could feel their eyes heating his skin so his cheeks burned. He should have been content with a simple hand-fasting ceremony. Just Emily and a couple of witnesses. This was an embarrassing mistake and all he wished to do was hide beneath the board, concealed by the tablecloth, and wait for the guests to eat their fill and be gone.

Just as he had that thought, he felt something brush his knee under the cloth. Then a small hand with dirty nails appeared between him and Emily.

'Master Seb, I ent had no breakfast,' came a wheedling whisper from beneath the table.

'Jack. What are you doing?'

'Me an' Beggar is 'ungry, ent we?'

Against his better judgement, Seb held a piece of roast boar meat under the table, felt fingers grasp it and then a hot, wet tongue was licking his hand. Oh no. Jack's little dog was also there, 'neath the laden board. A lunatic dog amongst trestles. Seb could foresee disaster.

A fine pottage of rabbit and chicken was served next and Jude pushed back his stool to stand and make an announcement.

'My lord, knights, citizens, friends and neighbours ... bearing in mind the nature of this occasion, when I placed my order with the poulterer for the coneys and fowls for this dish, I took the opportunity of arranging a surprise – one to remind the happy couple of their obligations to the future of mankind...' Jude paused to allow an outburst of cheering to die down. 'What could be more appropriate, recalling their fecundity, than live rabbits to entertain you?' Jude held up his hand and, at his signal, down by the font, Tom opened a basket, releasing a half dozen rabbits. The creatures scattered to all quarters of the church, hastening to hide themselves from so much noise, laughter and squeals of delight.

Seb had known nothing of Jude's surprise beforehand but he had a shrewd idea of how it would end.

Little Beggar, as fine a ratter and rabbiter as any dog in London, came bounding from beneath the table, barking furiously, followed by his scruffy young master, yelling for him to cease. As a particularly large buck rabbit dashed under the trestle board at the far end of the nave, Beggar was in hot pursuit. It was inevitable that chaos followed in haste behind. The trestle was knocked askew, the laden board teetered for uncounted moments before tipping sideways and crashing to the floor.

The bridegroom covered his face with his hands, awaiting the uproar, the curses and the extremes of embarrassment.

Instead, laughter erupted. It seemed most folk believed this was all part of the entertainment. Even Churchwarden Marlowe, his family and Stationer Henry Fabyan, who had had their bowls emptied on the floor of a sudden and their cups spilled, saw the funny side of it when Lord Richard ordered their cups refilled with best Gascon wine, at his expense. Beggar caught his rabbit and Father Thomas would have tufts of fur floating around in his vestry for weeks yet to come. There was merriment afresh as the children were given the task of catching the remaining five rabbits – all of which would find their way into someone or other's pottage pot – without Beggar's aid, he being tethered outside the church on Jude's orders. Jack was allowed to join the celebrations, under strict instructions from Jude to be quiet, or else.

'But first,' Jude told the lad, a finger wagging ominously, 'I would know how that livery collar came to be in your room. And don't try to put the blame on Tom either, for I won't bloody believe you, you little rascal. Well?'

'I wos on'y gonna polish it, wosn't I? I didn't want Master Seb to wear it all filfy, did I? So I went and tooked it las' night, t' clean it, but when I started rubbin' off the dirt, the gold cummed off an' all, didn't it? I didn't know wot t' do, so I hid it under Tom's stuff. I wos on'y tryin' to 'elp, wosn't I? Don't beat me, pleeease, master.'

'You deserve it, though, Jack. You're a bloody nuisance. But the beating can wait until tomorrow. Now behave yourself, if you can, and if you cannot, just stay away from me. Understand?'

'Aye, master.' Jack scampered off to join in the merry-making.

• •

When the feast was done, men hired for the day set to, removing the dishes to be washed and the guests dismantled the boards and trestles, stacking them in a side aisle, so the entertainment could begin. Folk took their stools and benches to the walls, sitting with friends and neighbours. Dame Ellen chatted with her fellow gossips and there was a good deal to be discussed: everyone wearing their Sunday best, the comparing of fashions and, not least, why young Sebastian was wearing the duke's livery collar; who was upon their exemplary behaviour and who was not. In particular, the women observed those who had already drunk more than their fair share of the free and plentiful wine and ale, Henry Fabyan being prominent among those unsteady on their feet and loud of voice.

Seb and Emily went among their guests, hand-in-hand, greeting each one by name with the bride doing most of the talking on behalf of her shy husband whose social graces, whilst not lacking, had never been much used. The happy couple approached a little group of stationers, Warden Collop and his wife and Henry Fabyan, among others. Warden Collop offered his congratulations to the groom with an excess of hearty back-slapping and Mistress Collop praised the bride's choice of colour for her bridal gown, its elegant cut and fine braid trimming. All the while, Henry Fabyan was staring at Seb, a glare quite brazen in its lack of manners.

'Why are you wearing that damned Yorkist collar, eh?' he demanded, speaking so loudly that other conversations ceased. 'Why is it you're not wearing my father's gold collar? 'Tis an insult to his memory and to the company he was so proud of. Where's the proper collar? What've you done with it, eh? I demand to know.'

'Best we don't discuss the matter here, Henry,' Warden Collop said, trying to soothe the noisy fellow.

Lord Richard and Sir Robert, upon hearing the words 'damned Yorkist', naturally moved closer to discover the source and reason for such ill-chosen words.

'No. We will discuss it here. Now,' Fabyan insisted, brushing aside the warden's calming hand. 'I demand to know.'

'Then we should go into the bell-tower,' Seb said, 'There we may have a little privacy.'

'Privacy be damned,' Fabyan roared. 'I would have you explain yourself, Foxley, before all these witnesses.' He swept his hand to indicate the guests, all of whom were now giving the little group of stationers their fullest attention.

'So be it,' Seb said, sighing. The last thing he wanted this day was any unpleasantness but it seemed now to be unavoidable. 'I assure you, Master Fabyan, that I had every intention of wearing your father's livery collar, as is the tradition. I had already paid the priest my one shilling for the privilege. However, the chain was soiled with candle soot and dust and was much in need of cleaning afore it could be worn to advantage and, upon removing the dirt...' Seb paused, bracing himself for the revelation. Someone put a cup in his hand and he drank the wine gratefully. 'As it was rubbed clean, I fear that we discovered, whereas the chain certainly was the colour of gold, that was all it was. The thin gold veneer flaked away, revealing base metal beneath. It pains me to say it, Master Fabyan, but your father's bequest is a fake.'

The guests gasped in unison.

'That's a lie. A confounded lie, Foxley,' Fabyan yelled. 'You've stolen the real chain and substituted a fake, so you can keep it for yourself. I know what you have done, you damned jackanapes.' Fabyan drew back his arm, bunching his fist to land a blow but Sir Robert was too fast and the stationer found himself in a painful grip that had him squirming.

'It is no lie and it can be proven,' Seb said. He turned to Jude, standing at his elbow. 'Would you fetch the chain from the church coffer, please, Jude. I fear Master Fabyan will not admit the truth without we lay bare the evidence.'

Jude brought the object in question and handed it to Seb, wondering what means his brother had in mind to prove the substitution had not been made so recently.

'Here, before these good people, I would prove that I am innocent of any deception,' Seb said, holding out the livery chain that anyone who wished to examine or touch it might do so. 'As you may see, where the thin layer of gold has been polished away, the base metal clearly shows through. Thus, there can be no doubt that this is not Sir Ralph Fabyan's collar so graciously bequeathed a decade since to the Stationers' Company for he would never have insulted the company by presenting them with some cheap and ill-made thing. I believe we can all agree to that?'

Seb allowed time for those present to confirm his words with nodding heads and disapproving frowns.

'And I may establish that I and mine played no part in exchanging the gold chain for this fake. Look to the inside of the links; see there the amount of dirt on the chain, the candle soot and thick dust which have accumulated. In this case, I would ask the womenfolk how long it would take for so much dirt to gather. Is it the grime of a few weeks, months or, maybe, years even?'

Dame Ellen, having looked closely and consulted with her friends, spoke for all.

'This is many years worth of filth, Master Sebastian. No half-decent housewife worthy of the name would permit such an accumulation to go undusted for so long. I would say 'tis a decade since it was last cleaned.'

'My thanks for the confirmation, good dame. In which case the presence of so much dirt proves the chain is not of recent making but has been in existence for many years, worn by other men at their nuptials without being dusted off. In fact, I would say it has never been cleaned since it came into the company's possession, proving that I and those of my household had nought to do with it, for we were but young lads ten years since. Had it not been for our Jack's enthusiastic polishing, the deception might have continued yet.'

Warden Collop stepped forward.

'And I recall the great fuss and to-do at the time when Sir Ralph's last will and testament was made known, when probate was granted at the Court of Hustings. I remember how Henry Fabyan here, as Sir Ralph's heir, contested his father's right to bequeath such a valuable object to the Stationers' Company, vehemently insisting on pursuing a legal case through the court. Then, of a sudden, he changed his mind regarding the legacy his father wished to make. The Master and Wardens of the Company were surprised at his change of heart – seemingly without explanation – but were much relieved that there would be no further unpleasantness in that regard.

'I believe we can now surmise why Henry Fabyan changed his mind. He had had a cheap copy of the chain made and it was this that he was content to have pass to the stationers. What may have become of the gold collar, we shall likely never know. What say you, Fabyan? Are the things spoken of by Master Foxley and myself not the truth? Did you have your father's collar melted down?'

'It was rightfully my inheritance' Fabyan blustered. 'My father had no right to give it away. It was his most valuable piece. He wasn't of sound mind when...'

'Indeed he was,' Warden Collop said, 'For I was among those who witnessed his signature that day.'

'Then you must have coerced him, forced him to...'

'No. It was his own decision.'

'Forgive my intrusion, warden,' Lord Richard said, 'But are we not here to celebrate the joining of Master Foxley and his bride in wedlock? Can company business not be settled upon another occasion?'

'Indeed, your grace. We beg pardon for our lack of courtesy.' The warden bowed low to the duke, 'But with your highness's permission, I would first remove this "offense" from the proceedings.' He took Henry Fabyan by the scruff of his gown.

'Certainly.' The duke grinned as Warden Collop shoved Fabyan towards the open church door and flung him into the street, dusting off his hands after.

• •

With the boards cleared away, the nave was made ready for an afternoon and evening of entertainment and revelry.

Jude, who had a fair talent for playing a pipe, had arranged for two of his friends, professional minstrels with the London Waits, to come with shawm, sackbut and curtal to provide music for the dancing.

Seb wasn't much of a one for step-dancing, having never learned because of his past difficulties when he had been so lame, though he thought at some future time, without an audience, he might try. No matter, he could most certainly sing and gave voice to some merry songs and carols, leaving the dancing to others.

Lord Richard was first among those to take the floor, performing a courtly measure with Dame Ellen, a common ring-dance with the bride, and a jig at the gallop, which involved exchanging partners as they swung around the nave. Breathless, everyone was keen to refresh themselves after so much exertion, making way for a troupe of jugglers, fire-eaters and sword-swallowers who dressed in strange exotic costumes and claimed to be Egyptians but, in fact, not one had been born farther afield than Stratford-atte-Bow. Their darkened skins were the result of judicious use of walnut juice and nought to do with the heat of distant lands. Even so, they were fine performers and brought the celebrations to a close. Apart from the final act, of course.

● ●

This was the part that Seb dreaded most. With the musicians leading the way, Seb and Emily were escorted from St Michael's the short distance along Paternoster Row to the Foxley house. Seb found Jude's smirk particularly unnerving. What japes and tricks had his brother planned? Herrings in the bed? Loosened bed ropes that would have them fall through the mattress? Mice trapped within the pillows? Anything was possible. Seb had pleaded with Jude not to insist on this customary part of the ceremony but he was just wasting words. Even Lord Richard had every intention of accompanying the couple to their bed. Nessie was giggling and skipping along, still strewing flower petals in front of Seb and Emily as the gathered throng led them to the bridal chamber.

The room was already full of people. Two expensive beeswax candles lit the gloom of the fading daylight. Jude pulled Seb through the crowd and numerous male hands – some inept in their enthusiasm and drunken state – began to unfasten the bridegroom's clothes and disrobe him. On the other side of the bed, Dame Ellen and her friends did the same for Emily, if somewhat more sedately.

The bed curtains had been tied back to reveal the stage where the couple would set the seal upon their union. The fine white sheets, a woven woollen counterpane and a fur coverlet – all part of the bride's dowry – were ready turned back. Nessie went to her task of sprinkling the bed with flowers and Father Thomas contributed a generous splashing of holy water, along with a Latin blessing. Emily might not know what was said but Seb felt his face redden as God was beseeched to make the groom potent and the bride fecund.

The chamber was already full, yet more folk came in, though they had manners enough to step aside, pressing into the walls to give passage to Lord Richard and Sir Robert. The bridal couple sat upon the bed, he wearing a white shirt, she a new shift, as the duke presented them with the gift of a silver-gilt loving cup, filled with warmed, spiced hippocras.

'You are a fortunate man, Master Sebastian,' the duke said. 'I wish you both a long, happy and fruitful union.' Then he withdrew, followed by Sir Robert, who added his own congratulations, and the priest. Seb and Emily sipped from their cup. She smiled at him over the rim. He almost managed to return the smile.

With such persons of rank no longer present to restrain the company, those who remained became ever more lewd. Young Jack was full of rude suggestions that belied his lack of years. Emily's brother, John, joined in with the innuendo and even Tom, the sober apprentice, made a few comments that had his master wanting to hide beneath the coverlet. Finally, thankfully, Jude took pity on the bridal pair and started to usher the crowd from the room.

'Get to work, little brother, 'tis your duty,' he said with a wink.

Seb sighed and rolled his eyes.

Dame Ellen came to the bride, whispered something quietly and placed a small item in her hand.

'In case you do not wish to conceive too soon,' she said.

Emily thanked the dame, but only half-heard the instruction and wasn't sure what the soft package in her hand was for.

• •

As soon as the last reveller was gone, Seb leapt out of bed and crawled beneath it.

'What are you doing, husband mine?' Emily asked, leaning over the edge of the bed to see Seb lying upon his back in the darkness underneath.

'Making sure Jude hasn't unknotted the ropes or put a herring or a dead mouse beneath the mattress to cause a stink.'

Emily laughed.

'He wouldn't do that,' she said.

'You don't know my brother so well as I. Believe me, he has done some mischief or other, I have no doubt. He mentioned the possibility of loosening the bed-ropes more than once. However, he seems not to have done so, praised be God.'

Seb returned to the bed to gaze upon his bride. Em wore her hair loose now. Like a cascade of molten copper and gold, it shimmered in the candlelight.

'Say it again, Em,' he whispered.

'Say what?'

'You called me "husband mine". I like the sound of that.'

'Well then, husband mine, I think we are supposed to do more than talk.'

'Plenty of time for that.'

'But don't you want to see what you have vowed to love and cherish before the candles burn down? My shift can be removed...'

'Are you not tired after such a day?'

'Not *too* tired. Yet it seems to me you are putting this off, Seb. 'Tis me who's supposed to be the reluctant virgin.'

32

'And you're not? Reluctant, I mean.'

'Help me with my shift, won't you? 'Tis cumbersome and I feel over hot.'

'Do you have a fever, Em? I can get you something...'

'I am perfectly well. Now help me get this off.'

Beneath her shift Emily's skin was pale as fresh milk, her breasts perfect, such that he finally realised he wanted to touch them. He reached out with nervous, gentle fingers to cup her breast. To the horror of them both, a black, sooty handprint now marred the whiteness of her flesh.

'Oh, Jude!' His brother had ruined the moment, just as Seb had feared, covering the ropes beneath the bed with soot. He felt like weeping with embarrassment but after a moment of shocked surprise, Em found it amusing.

She took his hands and daubed them all over them both, 'til their bodies were dirty with soot.

Laughing now, Seb and Emily lay alone in the bridal bed as the candles burnt down and made certain they were properly wed, as the law demanded and love desired.

## THE END

# *Historical note:*

The idea for this tale came while I was transcribing a fifteenth-century London will. I discovered a bequest of a livery chain to a London church to be displayed on a saint's statue for the use of bachelors of the parish to wear on special occasions, especially when they were wed – for a fee, of course.

The marriage, wedding breakfast and nuptials were inspired by a series of photographs from an authentic re-enactment of a medieval wedding at Archeon Living History Museum in the Netherlands.

The 'soft package' that Dame Ellen gave to Emily was probably a linen bag containing a small natural silk-sponge from the Mediterranean. Soaked in vinegar, these sponges were inserted as contraceptive devices in medieval times. Omitting the vinegar, they also made re-usable tampons.

I must also thank my husband Glenn for insisting that the story of Seb and Emily's marriage had to be told, following their adventures in *The Colour of Poison* and before their lives moved on to *The Colour of Cold Blood,* the second in the series of Sebastian Foxley Medieval Murder Mysteries from MadeGlobal Publishing.

## Toni Mount

Toni Mount earned her research Masters degree from the University of Kent in 2009 through study of a medieval medical manuscript held at the Wellcome Library in London. Recently she also completed a Diploma in Literature and Creative Writing with the Open University.

Toni has published many non-fiction books, but always wanted to write a medieval thriller, and her first novel "The Colour of Poison" is the result.

Toni regularly speaks at venues throughout the UK and is the author of several online courses available at www.medievalcourses.com.

# TONI MOUNT

A
Sebastian Foxley
Medieval
Murder Mystery

# THE COLOUR OF COLD BLOOD

# *Prologue*

H E GAZED at his handiwork and sighed. How sad. She'd been a beauty – once – but not now. He had enjoyed her company. On many a chilled night she'd warmed his bed and soothed his loneliness but, like all women, she had her faults, in particular, the inability to keep silent. That problem was solved forever now, he thought, wiping his soiled hands and the blade of his Irish knife on her linen shift, before concealing the weapon once more within his robes. He arranged her neatly, curled like a sleeping child, tidied her garments to preserve her modesty – not that she had bothered over much with such matters in life – nevertheless, she would be decent in death. No final confession for the likes of her, no last rites. Too bad. It was a task well done: at least one whore could lead the sons of Adam astray no more.

The pale, insipid moonlight cast the half-hearted shadow of the thorn hedge across the remains. Shaking his head, he left that unhallowed place. There was not a moment to lose; the solitary bell of St Michael's was already summoning the parishioners to the last service of the day, clanging like a cheap metal platter rapped with a spoon.

# *Chapter 1*

## Monday, the fourth day of November 1476, London

DAWN WAS breaking in the east, the rosy light shimmering on frosted roofs and walls, turning dirty old London to a place of magick and faery. Armed with his drawing implements and swathed in a grey woollen mantle, Sebastian Foxley stepped carefully along the frozen rutted ways of Panyer Alley and along the Shambles. There were few folk about so early. Greeted by the gatekeeper, still rubbing sleep from his eyes, Seb was the first to pass through Newgate as it opened for the day. He turned right up Giltspur Street towards Smithfield, inhaling the essence of the still-dormant city as it slumbered like a great beast, ready to awaken as the sun rose.

The late autumn grass, frost-rimed, crunched beneath his feet as he trudged towards his favoured spot beneath an oak tree, beside the Horse Pool. He noticed a good crop of oak galls attached to a low, leafless branch and collected a few, putting them in his purse. To a scrivener, they were as good as money for, together with a few rusty nails and a resin known as devil's fingernails, they made the best, blackest and longest lasting ink. He would send Tom and young Jack to collect more after dinner, then show them how to make the precious ink.

The hedgerow that ran alongside Chick Lane was aglow with jewels amongst the last yellowing leaves; each gem dusted with frost – haws and rosehips like rubies, sloes dark as sapphires, delicate-hued pearls of bryony. But his artist's eye was drawn to the diamond-strung cobwebs that draped the brambles. They could have graced a queen's throat if they did not disappear by dinnertime. He sketched quickly, capturing the beauty of a lacy leaf skeleton in the grass; a squirrel rummaging for acorns, flicking his rust-tinted tail and chittering a warning when he espied Seb invading his estate. He laughed at the little creature scolding him like a Billingsgate fishwife, and moved away. His fingers were chilled and he chafed a vestige of warmth into them so he might continue with the silver point, drawing a redbreast warbling his joyful hymn of praise to the new day from a spindle tree in the hedgerow. The bright-eyed bird might later adorn the margin of a Book of Hours Seb had in mind. The spindle tree flaunted its bright madder berries like a Winchester goose, parting her skirts to reveal nether garments vivid as sunset: the precious seeds within, glowing among the few remaining russet leaves.

The water of the Horse Pool held a wafer of ice around the rim, freezing the faded reeds in place, upright as sentinels. Not a whisper of wind disturbed the unfrozen water further out where a lone swan sat serenely upon her perfect reflection, the feathers of her folded wings gilt-edged by the strengthening light. Seb drew what he saw but only in his mind's eye could he lock away the memories, the nuances of colour, light and shadow. He spent time, capturing the swan in her glory, but the light was changing, becoming brazen, revealing the less than lovely. A broken bucket lay discarded in the hedge; the bones of a fox's kill strewn in the grass like white pot shards and a lost shoe, split at the heel. Frost on the oak tree began to thaw, an icy drip finding a gap betwixt his cap and mantle, shivering down his neck. The spell was broken and Seb made his way home. Chimneys were now smoking, window shutters opening as his

41

neighbours roused themselves to the day's labours; yawning and stretching and nodding a greeting as he passed by.

Just a few yards from Seb's door, a beggar sat hunched over his bowl, going through his beard, catching and cracking fleas between his thumbnails. A dusty heap of rags, he might have gone unnoticed, seeming more interested in fleas than collecting alms in his wooden dish, but Seb dropped in a groat all the same.

'God give ye good day, master.' The voice was hoarse and quavering.

'And also to you, Symkyn.'

## The Foxleys' house in Paternoster Row

THE HOUSE welcomed Seb with the delicious scents of fresh baked bread and frying bacon. Setting down his drawing stuff, he shrugged off his heavy mantle, hung it on the hook behind the door and went to the laver to wash his hands before eating. The warmth of the kitchen and the hot water thawed his blood quickly, setting his fingers tingling and flushing his cold-bleached nails with renewed colour.

A noisy company was already at the table. Jack sat on his bench, eager as a hatchling for the first mouthful, whatever, whenever, it came his way. Tom, the apprentice, was older but no less hungry, tapping the board with his spoon, eyes watching Mistress Emily dole generous helpings of savoury pottage into the wooden bowls stacked by the hearth to warm. Gabriel Widowson was perched on a stool, telling some tale of a drunken fool he'd seen last eve, but only Nessie, the serving wench, was listening as she gave him the largest helping of pottage, giggling.

'Nessie,' Seb interrupted, 'After we have eaten, take some fresh bread across the road to old Symkyn, and a piece of bacon. God knows he needs food more than we. Aye, even you, young Jack,' he said, seeing the look on the lad's face: fear that a mouthful due to him might go elsewhere. Not that Jack was greedy; no, just that his days as a starveling orphan weren't yet quite forgotten.

Seb kissed his goodwife on the cheek and whispered in her ear, smiling, before taking the stool at the head of the board. She more than returned the smile, her azure eyes bright with pleasure.

'Good day to you all,' Seb said. The others returned the greeting, spoons poised. 'Jack.'

The youngster looked sheepish, his spoon already plunged into the pottage, before grace was said. Seb recited the usual Latin prayer that Jack never understood, but the 'Amen' was clear enough: permission to eat.

Gabriel resumed his tale between mouthfuls, setting the lads spluttering with laughter into their breakfast but Emily and Seb had attention for naught but each other, exchanging knowing glances from either end of the board.

'No Jude this morning?' Seb asked, noting the empty place where his brother usually sat. It was always an awkward arrangement: Seb, though younger, was the married man and this his house, so he had the place at the head of the board, relegating Jude to a lesser position. For the most part, it didn't matter but sometimes Jude, usually on a bad day, took himself off to the Panyer tavern to eat. Perhaps this was one of those days. Sometimes it occurred to Seb that Jude might prefer to rent a place of his own, but neither of them had ever suggested it.

'Still abed, I dare say,' Gabriel answered. 'Heard him come home late last eve, later than me, even. He was singing some dirty ditty or other, stumbled on the stair. Reckon he was drunk. Probably still sleeping it off.' Gabriel sucked at his crooked front tooth, picking out a piece of bacon that had caught there. 'Hey, that was good pottage, Mistress Em, any chance of another helping?'

'You'll be as fat as a sow in furrow, you will, Gabriel,' Emily chided him, smiling, and turned away to see to the oatcakes on the griddle.

'Nonsense. Look at me.' Gabriel patted his muscular belly: flat as a platter.

The door from the yard opened, letting in a blast of icy air to announce Jude's arrival.

'You're late, as usual,' Emily said. 'Do it tomorrow and I'll give your breakfast to the pig. She deserves it more than you. Come next week, she'll pay for her keep, unlike some.' She slammed a platter of bacon collops, a bowl of pottage and two oatcakes on the board before her brother-in-law, flinging a spoon into the pottage so it splashed his tunic. He didn't seem to notice, saying nothing.

'Shall you be working for the coroner today, Jude?' Seb asked, referring to his brother's occasional employment by the city authorities.'

'Aye,' Jude replied, swallowing bacon, 'Have to assess the value of a knife. The Lord knows why. Some damn fool ran into another fellow as they were playing at football, skewered himself on the other's knife and bled to death. Since the king demands the value of the murderous weapon be paid as a fine for breaking the peace, I have the fool's task of discovering whether the knife was of a bladesmith's finest workmanship or a cutler's cheapest, made after dark.'

'I thought the guilds made it illegal to work after cock-shut, when none can see well enough to ensure high standards.'

'Supposedly.' Jude shoved the last collop into his mouth and put the second oatcake into his purse for later, leaving the pottage untasted. 'Not sure if I'll be back for dinner, or no.'

'Well that's not good enough,' Emily declared. 'How am I supposed to be sure not to waste food when I know not whether I shall be feeding you? I'm tired of you, Jude Foxley. You're more bother than a babe-in-arms. I shouldn't have to put up with it. Tell him, Sebastian.'

'Now, Em, don't take on so. Jude never knows what the coroner may ask of him...'

'I don't care. My entire day has to be arranged to suit your brother.'

'Then don't bother!' Jude yelled, shoving past her. 'I won't be back.'

'Oh, Em. Why is it you two cannot live amicably together? As if his moods are not dark enough, you upset him...'

'So it matters not that he upsets me with his wayward time-keeping, his sulks and his cup-shotten tantrums.'

'Come now, sweetheart, 'tis not so bad, surely?' Seb put his arm around her waist but she stepped out of his embrace.

'Not now. And why do you always take his side, making excuses for him?'

'I do not. Or I don't mean to. I love you, Em. I want you, only you.'

When breakfast was finally done, Seb sent Gabriel and the lads to the workshop to prepare for the day's work, before taking Emily in his arms. Oblivious of Nessie watching from the chimney corner, they kissed tenderly. Seb was loosening the pins in Emily's cap, the thought of her autumnal tresses cascading freely quickened his breath as she pressed closer. Jude chose that moment to return. The happy couple pulled apart, guilty of a stolen moment. Seb clenched his fists and with the briefest gesture of both greeting and farewell, hurried towards the workshop, overcome by a hot rush of blood to his cheeks.

'Now what?' Emily demanded.

'Forgot my scrip,' Jude said, then called out after Seb, 'Though plainly some people have matters other than a day's work on their minds, eh, little brother?'

'You're disgusting. We *are* married, after all,' Emily said, straightening her apron and patting her cap back in place. Suddenly she had her broom – her favoured weapon – in his face. 'Get out of my kitchen!' She jabbed the business end of cut reeds at his chest, 'And there'll be no dinner for you this morning, nor supper tonight if you can't be on time. Just go away.'

Jude withdrew from his sister-in-law's temper to join his brother in the workshop. Seb sat at his desk, his inks and brushes ready set out, but he was frowning at nothing.

'Ah, so that's it, is it? A row and now you have to make amends, eh? What was it about? Money? Sex? It's always one or the other.'

'Neither. Why is it you have to make lewd remarks every time I so much as look at my goodwife. Just because you're not wed...'

'I've got more bloody sense.'

'Keep out of our affairs, Jude! Leave us alone, can't you?' Seb's anger was all but unknown in the workshop.

Jack, Tom and Gabriel kept their heads down so low their noses near touched their desks, feigning deafness.

Jude shrugged.

'Have it your own way then. What do I care?' He turned aside, selecting a new quill and taking out his knife to cut and prepare the point but then he threw it down and stomped out. Off to his other – and at present – more amicable employment with the coroner.

## The Foxleys' parlour

'THE LORD bishop, in his wisdom, thinks I need help in my parish, though the Lord knows I must be twenty years younger than his grace... well, ten at least.' Father Thomas, the priest at St Michael le Querne in Cheapside, sighed deeply as he sank into the chair, grateful for the cushions Mistress Foxley provided, aye, and the good ale. He glanced around the comfortable room, smiling when he saw the elegant silver-gilt loving cup upon the shelf, a wedding gift to the Foxleys from the Duke of Gloucester, reminding the priest of that merry occasion a year past. 'But there you are,' he continued. 'Who am I to argue? I'm getting an assistant and there's an end to it. I am informed that the new man is most diligent about his duties.' The old priest puffed out his cheeks. 'Not too diligent, I trust. Don't

46

want him upsetting my parishioners, do we? Some of them are quite set in their ways.'

'I'm sure you'll keep his enthusiasm within bounds, father,' Emily said, offering the priest a smile and another almond wafer.

'I hope so but a new broom sweeps clean, as my mother, God rest her dear soul, used to say.' He made the sign of the cross with gnarled old fingers and Emily did the same. 'Bishop Kemp insists he will seek out the roots of Lollard heresy wherever they may be found. Well, he'll be wasting his time at St Michael's in that case: none of my parishioners would dabble in that wicked nonsense, I can tell you.'

'Of course not. Why would the bishop think...'

'I don't know, my dear, some rumours about Gospel books in English circulating in the city. Well, that may be so, but not in my parish. My people, including you and your goodman, are all honest, God-fearing folk, obedient to the Holy Father in Rome. No question of that.'

'No question at all. More ale, father? Now what was it you wanted to see my Sebastian about? A new book, did you say?'

The old priest nodded, his tonsure a halo of wispy white hair encircling his skull cap. He reached for another wafer.

'Aye, what was it now? Mm, a psalter book, aye. I doubt my new assistant will want to share my ancient volume, seeing it's falling apart with age.'

'Sebastian could repair it. I'm sure he'd do it at a most reasonable price for you, as a friend.'

'Mm, most kind, but this new fellow – Weasel, or whatever his name is...'

'Weasel? That's a quaint name, isn't it?' Emily said, hiding a grin behind her hand.

'Well, something of the sort. He'll expect a new psalter at least, I don't doubt. Not that St Michael's can really afford it.'

'I'll fetch Sebastian from the workshop, so you may discuss it with him, here, in comfort.'

Emily bustled out, leaving Father Thomas seated before the hearth. Content, he helped himself to the last wafer, leant back upon the cushions and closed his eyes, thinking what a well-ordered, pleasant and pious household the Foxleys kept.

In the workshop, Master Seb wasn't looking his usual, cheerful self. Jack didn't know what was amiss but he didn't like bad feeling in the house for all too often, in his old life, other people had tended to vent their ill-humours on him. At least in the Foxley household, usually Master Jude was the only one who might do that but this morning Master Seb had a thunderous scowl upon his face. Jack's dog had made a mess in the middle of the workshop floor, not for the first time.

'Jack. I've told you before about...'

'Sorry, master, but Little Beggar's profleegate, ain't he?'

'What? Where did you learn that?'

'From you, Master Seb. Last week, you said the mayor was too profleegate with his coin, now he's got a new wife.'

'Hush, will you.'

'That's what you said. And Little Beggar's profleegate wiv his shit: spreadin' it all around.'

'Well, get it cleared up. I can't have the workshop reeking like a cess pit and customers treading in the muck all day.'

Jude, lately returned from interviewing various cutlers and bladesmiths on the coroner's behalf, left off sewing together the leaves of a new book and came to add his pennyworth, hands on hips:

'I've told you the same often enough, you little wretch. This time that bloody dog's for drowning. You hear me?'

'But he don't mean no trouble. Please don't drowned him, pleease.'

'No one's going to drown anything,' Seb said, seeing the lad on the verge of tears. Jude was always upsetting him about that blessed dog.

'You speak for yourself, Seb. I'm sick and tired of the damned thing. If I have to step around its piles of shit and puddles of piss once more...'

Jack was sobbing now.

'Leave it, Jude, for pity's sake. I'm too weary for this. I have to go down to Queenhithe, see what's happening about our cargo from Captain Marchmane. The *St Christopher* docked on Saturday yet we've heard nothing about the paper and pigments the captain was bringing in for us. Meantime, Jack! Clean up the mess and we'll say no more of the matter.'

'Until the next bloody time,' Jude added with a malicious look in his eye.

Seb went to his work desk, leafing through the sketches he had done by the Horse Pool that morning. Little Beggar came trotting over to him, sat on his haunches and raised his front paw. Whatever the Church said about creatures having no souls, with dolorous brown eyes looking up him, pleading, Seb could almost doubt the wisdom of the pronunciation. If that dog wasn't begging forgiveness for his sins... Seb found himself with a moist eye, scratching Beggar's scruffy little head. The dog's tail thumped the flagstones, as if he understood he was half-way to being pardoned for his crime. Jack was just finishing his unsavoury task.

'Take him over to Smithfield, Jack. You can collect those oak apples I told you about whilst Beggar may redeem himself and bring back a coney for the pot.'

'Aye, Master Seb.' Jack didn't need telling twice.

'Thought you were going to Queenhithe,' Jude said. 'Why don't you take one of these idle devils with you?' He nodded towards Gabriel and Tom. 'Christ knows why we employ either of them. When was the last time you moved your lazy backside, eh, Gabe?'

Gabriel Widowson gave a wry grin. He was not a handsome young man with his mousy hair and mismatched eyes – one blue, the other brown – and a lopsided mouth with a crooked tooth, yet his air of self-belief inspired confidence. Folk liked Gabriel without being able to say quite why. The rumour ran that he was the natural son of some person of rank, though whether bishop or baron depended on who told the tale and he did nothing to quell the rumours. In fact, he tended to encourage them with a knowing look, a wink, enjoying the harmless notoriety.

He had been the subject of endless hours of gossip around the conduit and at the back of St Michael's church on a Sunday for months, ever since the Foxleys had taken him on as a journeyman scrivener and illuminator at Paternoster Row last summer. Wenches were drawn like iron to a lodestone by the mystery surrounding this incomer from Kent. At least, that was where he claimed to have come from and he spoke like a man of that county. But some wondered when he told tales of Scotch moss-troopers and Irish slavers, Breton pirates and Moorish potentates. Gabriel was a gifted spinner of stories but which were true and which invented, none could tell. Like the rumours of his paternity – son of a prince or a pauper – somehow it didn't matter.

Gabriel laughed, seeing Jude scowling at him. There was no point in taking offence. It was just Jude's way. The journeyman set down his pen and closed the exemplar he had been copying from – a complex Latin treatise concerning the Old Testament biblical text of Leviticus, ordered by Thomas Kemp, the Bishop of London. It was a tedious task indeed, the text of uninspiring Latin did naught to raise Gabriel's spirit and he was glad to set it aside.

'Oh, I seem to recall doing a little work a week or two since, naught too exhausting. Why? What would you have me do?'

'Go with my brother to Queenhithe. He may need assistance to carry our reams of new paper. Oh, and see you keep him from the local brothels.' Jude, in better humour now, gave a snort at the thought of his straight-laced brother ever visiting a whore-house.

Just as Seb and Gabriel were taking down their cloaks from the hooks by the door, Emily hurried in.

'Oh, Seb,' she said, 'Father Thomas is here, in the parlour. I said you would speak to him about a new psalter book he needs for an assistant priest who is joining St Michael's. Could you see him now? He seems to think the need is quite urgent.'

Seb nodded, sighing.

'Aye. Of course. My thanks, Em. Tell him I'm coming,' he called as Emily returned to the parlour. 'Tom, fetch the pattern book for me and bring it along.' Seb turned to Gabriel. 'Our errand will have to wait until after dinner,' he said, removing his cloak.

'Or I could go alone?' Gabriel offered.

'Do you know the *St Christopher* out of Deptford? She has a bright blue and gold painted prow – a newish caravel.'

'I'll find her. What did we order?'

'A dozen reams of Bruges paper, water-marked with a hound's head, and a box of finest Venice pigments that Captain Marchmane promised he would bring. 'Tis all paid for in advance. If everything has been off-loaded from the ship, try the Customs House. You know where that is? Beyond the bridge, passed Billingsgate, in Water Lane, by the Wool Quay.'

'Fear not, Master Seb, I know the Customs House. I've lived in London long enough to learn my way around, even if I wasn't born here, like you.' In truth, he thought, I probably know the shadier parts of the city better than you do. But he smiled his lopsided smile and left, going out into the chill November street. Old Symkyn was still there, hunched behind his begging bowl, watching the world pass by, all but invisible.

• •

Over supper that eve, as the daylight was fading and the tapers were lit, Seb told the others about the new commission of a psalter book for St Michael's.

'I-I told Father Thomas we would make the book for him *gratis*.'

'What's gratis?' Jack asked.

'You did what!' Jude spluttered gravy on the cloth. 'How do you expect us to make a living, you dolt? We can't afford such generosity.'

'It will be good for our souls...'

'Bugger souls, Seb. I want a roof over my head and food on the bloody board. How dare you decide to do it for naught without my agreement?'

'I apologise, Jude. I thought you would wish to...'

'Well, I don't. Church robs enough from my purse in tithes as it is without you giving them weeks of work and expensive stuff for free. I suppose you intend to use gold embellishment?'

Seb nodded.

'Just a little, maybe.'

'You know they won't let us off a pennyworth of tithes in return. They're worse than leeches, sucking us dry.' Jude was wringing his napkin so fiercely the linen began to tear.

'It will be a fine opportunity to use those new pigments... when I receive them, eh, Gabe?' Seb tried to turn the conversation but realised that the mention of using expensive colours on the psalter was a mistake. 'How come you did not fetch them?'

'I went to the *St Christopher,* as you said,' Gabe replied. 'She was half unloaded already. I asked about your colours but the mate, Raff Scraggs, knew naught of them. Then I asked to speak with your friend, Captain Marchmane. Raff, I mean, Master Scraggs, said they hadn't seen the captain since soon after they docked on Saturday eve, so I couldn't ask him, could I?' Gabe returned his attention to his trencher, keen to get on with the succulent pig's trotter and peas in a good thick gravy.

'And our reams of paper? What of those?'

'Seb.' Emily interrupted, 'Can we discuss work after we have eaten, afore the food goes cold upon the platters?'

'This is important. We are short of good quality paper. That French stuff is thin and poorly made. Good enough for the lads to practise upon but not for the likes of Father Thomas's new psalter. I want the best for a Church book. So where is it, Gabe?'

'Fear not. It's at the Customs House, I made sure. We should have it by Wednesday, Thursday at the latest. You know how long such matters take, what with documents to be sealed, duties paid, tallies noted and all.'

'What else is fer supper, mistress?' Jack asked, pushing aside his trencher, cleaned down to the bare wood.

'Don't interrupt, Jack,' Seb said, rapping the board with his knife handle. 'This is business and you become more inconsiderate by the day. Now keep silent at table unless we speak to you.'

'Wot's 'inconseedrite' mean, Tom?' Jack whispered to his fellow apprentice, seated beside him on the bench.

'Do you understand what 'keep silent' means, Jack?'

'Aye, Master Seb.' For a moment Jack looked downcast but his eyes brightened like sunrise as Emily set a baked apple before him, stuffed with raisins and spiced sugar.

'At least one among you appreciates the food I spend all day preparing,' she said, jogging Seb's elbow, meaningfully. 'I believe you would hardly notice if I served you raw giblets and mouldy horse bread for every meal. Why do I go to so much effort, I wonder?'

'Because 'tis a woman's place,' Jude said without looking at his sister-in-law.

Everyone at table held their breath, expecting the worst. Mistress Emily and Master Jude rarely saw eye to eye as it was. Like fire and gunpowder, their near encounter could cause untold destruction.

'Supper is excellent, as always, sweetheart,' Seb said, hoping to diffuse the tension but Emily ignored him.....

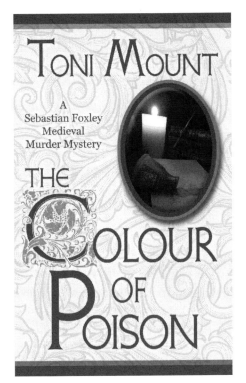

TONI MOUNT

A
Sebastian Foxley
Medieval
Murder Mystery

THE

COLOUR

OF

POISON

978-84-944893-3-4

**The first Sebastian Foxley
Medieval Mystery by Toni Mount.**

The narrow, stinking streets of medieval London can sometimes be a dark place. Burglary, arson, kidnapping and murder are every-day events. The streets even echo with rumours of the mysterious art of alchemy being used to make gold for the King.

Join Seb, a talented but crippled artist, as he is drawn into a web of lies to save his handsome brother from the hangman's rope. Will he find an inner strength in these, the darkest of times, or will events outside his control overwhelm him?

Only one thing is certain - if Seb can't save his brother, nobody can.

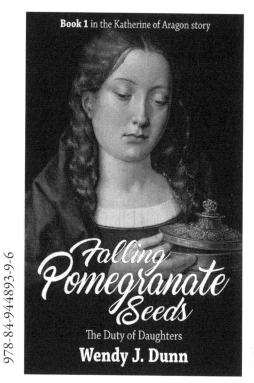

978-84-944893-9-6

**Book 1 in the Katherine of Aragon Story**

Doña Beatriz Galindo.
Respected scholar.
Tutor to royalty.
Friend and advisor to Queen Isabel of Castile.

Beatriz is an uneasy witness to the Holy War of Queen Isabel and her husband, Ferdinand, King of Aragon. A Holy War seeing the Moors pushed out of territories ruled by them for centuries.

The road for women is a hard one. Beatriz must tutor the queen's youngest child, Catalina, and equip her for a very different future life. She must teach her how to survive exile, an existence outside the protection of her mother. She must prepare Catalina to be England's queen.

A tale of mothers and daughters, power, intrigue, death, love, and redemption. In the end, Falling Pomegranate Seeds sings a song of friendship and life.

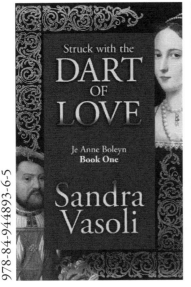
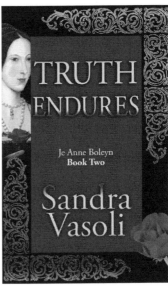

978-84-944893-6-5

978-84-944893-7-2

The *Je Anne Boleyn* series is a gripping account of Anne Boleyn's effort to negotiate her position in the treacherous court of Henry VIII, where every word uttered might pose danger, where absolute loyalty to the King is of critical importance, and in which the sweeping tide of religious reform casts a backdrop of intrigue and peril.

Anne's story begins with *Struck with the Dart of Love*: Tradition tells us that Henry pursued Anne for his mistress and that she resisted, scheming to get the crown and bewitching him with her unattainable allure. Nothing could be further from the truth.

The story continues with *Truth Endures*: Anne is determined to be a loving mother, devoted wife, enlightened spiritual reformer, and a wise, benevolent queen. But others are hoping and praying for her failure. Her status and very life become precarious as people spread downright lies to advance their objectives.

The unforgettable tale of Henry VIII's second wife is recounted in Anne's clear, decisive voice and leads to an unforgettable conclusion...

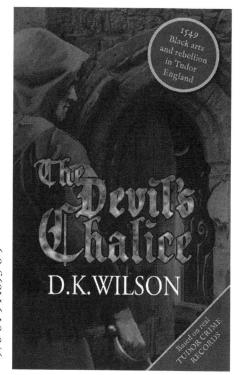

### The Real Crime

In the steaming summer of 1549 two men languish in the Tower of London. William West is accused of attempted murder. Robert Allen is under investigation for dabbling in the Black Arts. Meanwhile, England is in the grip of rebellions against the boy king, Edward VI. The connections between these facts remains a mystery.

### Our Story

London goldsmith, Thomas Treviot, is sent by his patron, Archbishop Cranmer, to discover discreetly what connections West has with leading figures at court. But Thomas has problems of his own: his teenage son has gone off to Norwich to join rebels led by Robert Kett. Trying to find his son and please Cranmer, he is plunged into dangers from peasant mobs, London gangsters and political chicanery, not to mention an enemy wielding occult power...

Once again, D.K. Wilson bases his story on documented facts in order to evoke the feverish atmosphere of 1549's 'summer of discontent' in which magic was as real to people as mob violence and political scheming.

## Non Fiction History

Anne Boleyn's Letter from the Tower - **Sandra Vasoli**
Queenship in England - **Conor Byrne**
Katherine Howard - **Conor Byrne**
The Turbulent Crown - **Roland Hui**
Jasper Tudor - **Debra Bayani**
Tudor Places of Great Britain - **Claire Ridgway**
Illustrated Kings and Queens of England - **Claire Ridgway**
A History of the English Monarchy - **Gareth Russell**
The Fall of Anne Boleyn - **Claire Ridgway**
George Boleyn: Tudor Poet, Courtier & Diplomat - **Ridgway & Cherry**
The Anne Boleyn Collection - **Claire Ridgway**
The Anne Boleyn Collection II - **Claire Ridgway**
Two Gentleman Poets at the Court of Henry VIII - **Edmond Bapst**

## Historical Fiction

Falling Pomegranate Seeds - **Wendy J. Dunn**
Struck With the Dart of Love - **Sandra Vasoli**
Truth Endures - **Sandra Vasoli**
Phoenix Rising - **Hunter S. Jones**
Cor Rotto - **Adrienne Dillard**
The Raven's Widow - **Adrienne Dillard**
The Claimant - **Simon Anderson**
The Truth of the Line - **Melanie V. Taylor**

## Children's Books

All about Richard III - **Amy Licence**
All about Henry VII - **Amy Licence**
All about Henry VIII - **Amy Licence**
Tudor Tales William at Hampton Court - **Alan Wybrow**

# PLEASE LEAVE A REVIEW

If you enjoyed this book, *please* leave a review at the book seller
where you purchased it. There is no better way to thank the
author and it really does make a huge difference!
*Thank you in advance.*

Printed in Great Britain
by Amazon